Crabby's Water Wish

HAPPY READING!

This book is especially for:

Suzanne Tate,
Author—
brings fun and
facts to us in her
Nature Series.

James Melvin,
Illustrator—
brings joyous life
to Suzanne Tate's
characters.

Suzanne and James in costume

Crabby's Water Wish
A Tale of Saving Sea Life
Suzanne Tate
Illustrated by James Melvin

Nags Head Art
Number 9 of SUZANNE TATE'S NATURE SERIES

To HUMANS everywhere
who work for clean water
Thanks!
— Crabby & Nabby

1992
<u>NATIONAL AWARD WINNER</u>

Crabby's Water Wish was an award winner in
the National Federation of Press Women's 1992
Communications Contest.

Library of Congress Control Number 91-60262
ISBN 1-878405-04-7
ISBN 978-1-878405-04-3
Published by
Nags Head Art, Inc., P.O. Drawer 1809, Nags Head, NC 27959

Crabby and Nabby were two happy crabs.
They lived in shining waters
at a place called Green Island.

Green Island was a pleasant place.
In the waters around it,
there were safe places for sea life.

Baby sea life could grow and hide there.
It was like a nursery.
Crabby and Nabby liked to live there.

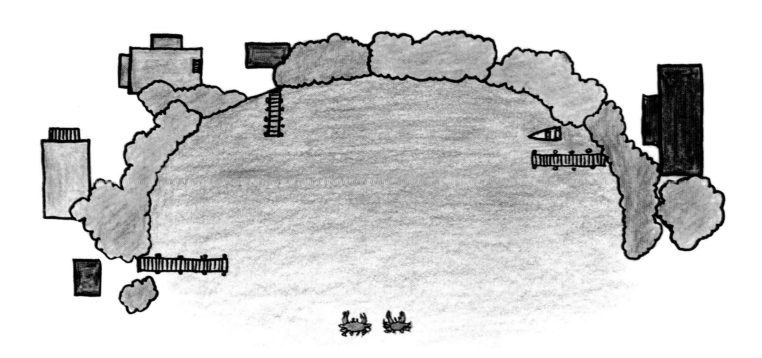

"Isn't the water nice today?"
Crabby would say to Nabby.
And Nabby would wave a claw
and wiggle her backfin.
(It was her way of nodding yes!)

Many kinds of sea life swam and ate
in the waters around Green Island.

One day, Crabby said to Nabby —
"Let's go fishing for food near the Little Bridge."
"That's a good idea!" replied Nabby.
And they flipped their backfins
and swam along in the water.

Soon they came to the Little Bridge,
where FISHERMEN could catch careless spots.

"Oh, there's Spunky Spot!" said Nabby.
"And Billy Bluefish swimming
like a big blue bullet!"

Swimming sea life swirled
around the Little Bridge.
Crabby and Nabby could find
plenty of fish to eat.

Later, they swam to the bottom where a bed of oysters lived.
"I wonder how Pearlie Oyster and her bedfellows
are doing," said Nabby.
"Since the water is nice and clean,
they are just fine," replied Crabby.
"Each one of them has its mouth open a tiny bit —
just enough to strain the water for food."

Suddenly, Crabby and Nabby
saw a great stirring of sea life!

"What is going on?" asked Crabby.
Nabby saw a big blob in the water.
"Why, it's Mary Manatee," she said.

The swirling sea life was scared!
But Nabby told them, "Don't be afraid!

Mary Manatee is a gentle giant.
She likes only plants and will not hurt or eat you.
She is just trying to stay away from BOATS!"

Crabby and Nabby swam back to Green Island.
It was then that they saw Lucky Lookdown!
He popped up beside an old tire lying on the bottom.
"Oh, I'm tired of trash like that," said Nabby.
"Humans shouldn't throw in the water
things they don't want."

Crabby and Nabby swam around the old tire.
But the water seemed not as clear as before.
Nabby could hardly see.
She bumped into a crab pot on the bottom.
It was an old "runaway" pot.
(A FISHERMAN had lost track of it in a storm.)

All of a sudden, Nabby was trapped
in that pot!

Crabby followed Nabby.
"Let me help you!" he said.
But then he was caught too.

Nabby was scared.
She saw something move.

But it was just Sammy Shrimp!
He zipped right through a hole in the pot.
Crabby and Nabby followed him.

As the days passed,
the water became
more and more murky and muddy.
It looked sick!
Rain had been running
off the bare land —
bringing soil and mud
to Crabby's and Nabby's home.

Crabby and Nabby were having trouble.
They could not get enough oxygen
from the water.
Crabby sighed sadly, "How I wish the
water would be clean again."

About that time, Flossie Flounder came along.
She was having trouble too.
Flossie was swimming along the top of the water
near the shore — trying to get more oxygen.

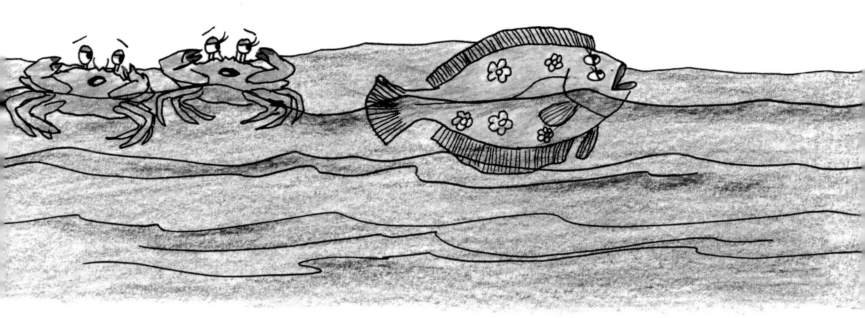

Then Crabby and Nabby did the same thing.
It was almost like all of them
were walking on the water!

A teacher and her class
came by to look at Green Island.
They were on a field trip.
Clean Water Charlie was with them!
He had been talking to the children
about saving sea life.

"Oh, there are some crabs and a flounder
trying to get more oxygen," Clean Water Charlie said.
"That is called a 'flounder walk.'"
The children were sorry
to see the suffering sea life.
"What can we do to help?" they asked.

"Let's go home and study ways
for all of us to help,"
Clean Water Charlie said.

"And we will write letters
to our leaders —
asking their help
in cleaning up the water."

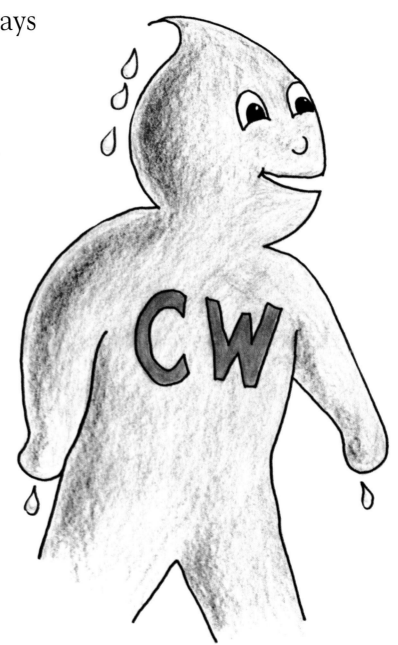

Back home, Clean Water Charlie showed the children
ways to save sea life.

They planted trees and grass
to hold the soil.
They made posters showing proper care
of poisons.
And they wrote letters to the leaders who make laws.

Meanwhile, Crabby and Nabby decided
to swim to Buzzard's Bay.
(It was a large bay where they might live better.)
As they swam past the Little Bridge,
they saw that Pearlie Oyster was doing poorly.

"Poor Pearlie," said Nabby.
"Her mouth is wide open.
She is trying to get more oxygen.
It's too bad she has to stay in one place
and can't go with us."

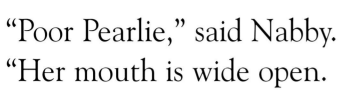

Buzzard's Bay did prove to be
a better place for Crabby and Nabby.
But they became homesick!
They swam back to Green Island a year later.
Crabby was surprised and happy to see
that the water was clear.
He didn't know how hard everyone
had worked to clean it up.

Standing again beside the water
were the children and their teacher.
Clean Water Charlie was there too.
All of them waved and shouted —

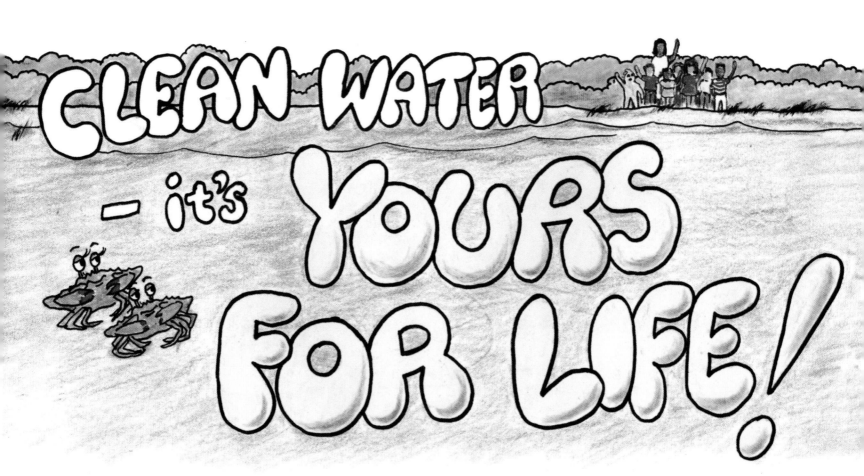

Crabby was glad to see them.
He didn't know what they were saying —
but he had his wish!
All was well for all of the sea life.
The water was clean and clear once again!